Mr. Cthulhu Presents:

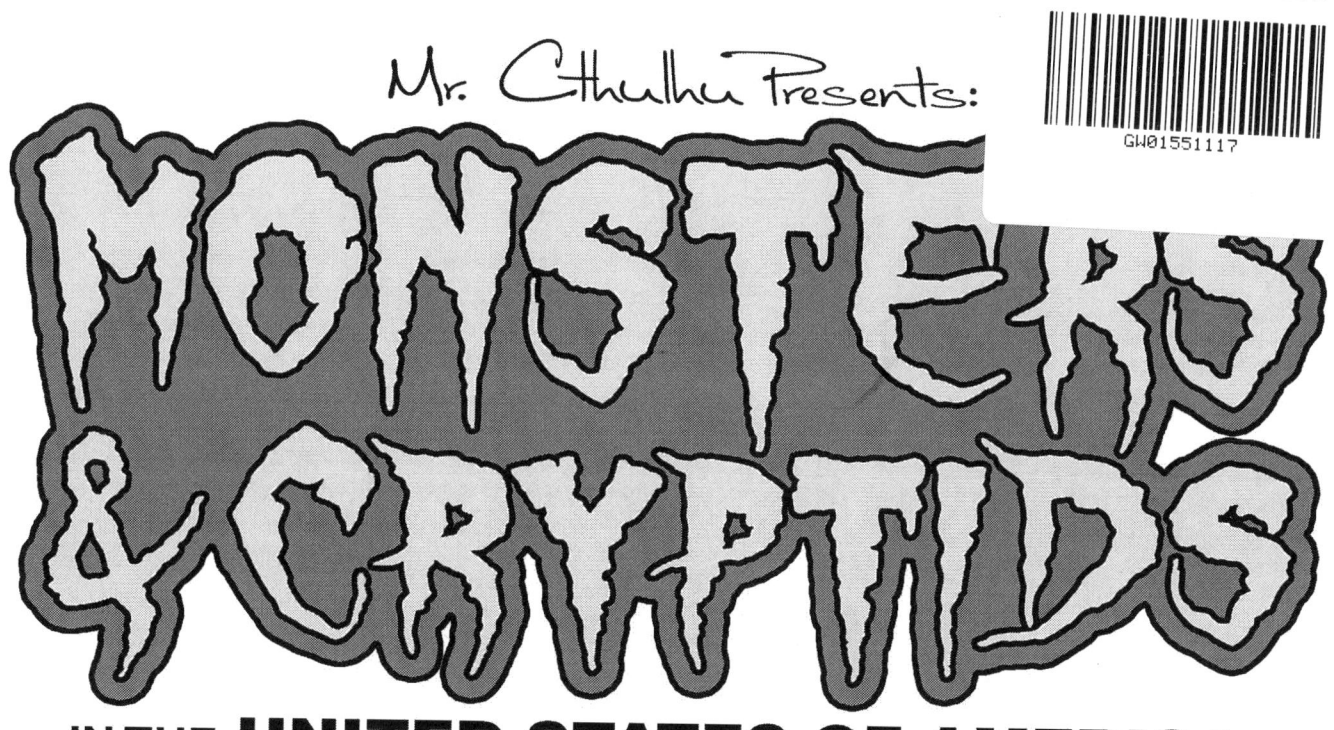

IN THE **UNITED STATES OF AMERICA**

COLORING BOOK
Illustrations by Phil Velikan

Mr. Cthulhu Presents:
Monsters and Cryptids in the United States of America

All rights reserved under International and Pan-American Copyright Conventions

Layout, cover and illustrations by Phil Velikan www.FindPhil.com
Edited by Holly Kondras
Back cover coloring by Mitchell Velikan

Printed in the United States of America

Published by VIG Publishing 2017

Table of Contents

Monsters and Cryptids in the United States of America

This book is a labor of love, a collection of creatures I grew up hoping to someday see, and a few creatures newly discovered while researching this book.

I remember watching *In Search Of...* with Leonard Nimoy when I was ten or so. That show started my fascination with all things creepy and mysterious. I was a farm kid who read horror story collections, watched *Tales From the Dark side* and bought comics like *The House of Mystery* and *The Unexpected.* It fascinated me that there might be creatures out there in my family's woods that were hidden from the eyes of men.

My son recently discovered Bigfoot, Nessie and other cryptids, which led me to wonder if each state had it's own special sightings of things unknown to science. I'm not talking about legends and folklore, I'm talking about things people actually have seen and reported.

I started looking through books and combing the internet. I soon discovered that a few states have over a dozen different creatures that have been spotted in their territory while others have almost no sightings of the cryptid kind whatsoever.

So I had a little work to do.

I've selected one Monster to represent each state. I cross-referenced creature sightings so that there would be no duplicates in the book. If two states had a giant turtle, but one of those also had something else that was interesting, I went with the something else. There was give and take for several states to have something of their own, but I think I achieved it. Also, I avoided including (but am collecting) non-cryptids such as aliens and ghosts as there are enough of those to warrant their own coloring books.

This was a fun book to author, and all of the cryptids and craziness included here can be found on the internet just by googling the creatures' names. Go, dig deeper, this is just a jumping off point for you to enjoy what could be out there... **in the dark**.

Wolf-woman of Mobile Alabama 1971

On April 8, 1971, the newspapers of Mobile, Alabama reported that they had received over 50 phone calls in the course of a week, reporting the sighting of a wolf-woman. Police had also been called to investigate sightings of a woman that was part wolf. Dozens of witnesses described her as having the torso of a beautiful woman and the hind quarters of a wolf. She allegedly ran on all fours and was "pretty and hairy." No one was assaulted, but the police took the story seriously due to the sheer number of phone calls.

Illiamna Lake Monster Alaska 1942-Present

In 1942, Babe Alyesworth flew over Illiamna lake and reported seeing dozens of dull aluminum colored fish with broad blunt heads, and bodies that were about 20 feet long. The massive creatures' tails moved side to side, unlike whales. Reports of these "fish" continued in the 1950s, and in 1967 a man used stainless steel cables attached to tuna hooks to catch something that then dragged his pontoon plane around the lake. When the plane was released, three cables were gone and the 8-inch hooks that remained were pulled straight.

Devil Monkeys **Arizona** 1934-Present

Often mistaken for kangaroos because of their upright stance and powerful back legs, Devil Monkeys have been seen from Arizona to Virginia. Baboon-like creatures, they seem to be 4-5 feet tall, have a long bushy tail and three-toed feet. They are described as fairly shaggy all over with tiny pointed ears atop a canine face. They have smaller front limbs but can leap across fields with suprising speed and agility. Several reports have them attacking cars and trying to get to the people inside.

Ozark Black Howler Arkansas 1846-Present

First encountered in Red Oak and later at Devil's Den, the Howler is typically described as being a "bear-sized" cat, with a thick body, stocky legs, black shaggy hair, red glowing eyes and horns. It stands between 3 and 4 feet at the shoulder. All reports say it has dark colorings, and long hair along the jawline. Its cry is said to be a combination of a wolf's howl and an elk's bugle. Reports of hearing the cry far outnumber the sightings, the most recent of which was near Lake Springdale in Benton County, Arkansas in 2016!

The final entry in the Fr. Martinez journal stated: "My God. My God. They are all gone. The winged demons have risen! What sin have we committed against each other and thy sacred earth? May the forgiving Lord not abandon their souls, which were taken from them into the depths of hell! Despite the earthly fires of man, a sole tree remained on the mountain's peak. And the Devils that spared me, returned to the refuge of that Lone Pine of the Mountain."

CALIFORNIA

Lone Pine Mountain Devil California 1878-Present

Father Justus Martinez wrote in his journal that one night while journeying west with 36 other Spanish settlers, he placed his small tent on the outskirts of the larger camp for privacy. In the late hours of the night the camp was ferociously attacked by "winged demons," leaving him as the only survivor. The Mountain Devils are said to be bat-like, large, furry and multi-winged, with claws and several layers of fangs. They are said to eat only the soft cartilage of the face, head and torso.

River Dinosaurs Colorado 1982-Present

Many reports have circulated about creatures that look like lizards running on two legs. They are described as being about three feet tall and five feet long, including the 24 inch tail. The term "River Dinosaur" relates to the fact that the sightings are always in areas with standing or running water. The creatures reportedly move swiftly and gracefully on skinny bird-like legs and have cone-shaped snouts. Lower down, they have arm-like apendages that seem to come from their long necks rather than the body.

Melon Heads Connecticut 1600s-Present

Colonial-era witches banished from a settlement? A fierce race of cannibals? Patients from a mental hospital that burned down in 1960? There are centuries worth of Melon Head stories and sightings. Whatever the origin, these creatures may have sought refuge in the harsh Connecticut woods and started preying upon local hikers. They are seen as small humanoids with huge heads, bulging eyes and spindly limbs that attack, bite and consume anyone caught crossing into their territory.

Selbyville Swamp Monster Delaware 1920-Present

Great Cypress Swamp holds a secret. In 1920 raccoon hunters were chased from the swamp when their dogs "tucked tail and ran" from something large, heavy and screaming. For 40 years, reports continued to come in about the swamp monster. In 1964 two men made a monster costume and haunted the area. They were forced to quit when they realized their lives were in danger from monster hunters. The men stopped, yet the reports keep coming in.

Gatormen Florida 1700s-Present

The Everglades have been rumored to be the home of smart, razor-toothed hominids for hundreds of years. Approximately five-feet long with a muscular tail, these cryptids have stubby gator-legs, a child-sized torso and alligator-like heads. Covered in thin greenish scales with webbed fingers and toes, the creatures are said to have reason and tool building skills as well as a grunting language to help them coordinate their attacks upon anything that stumbles into their swamp.

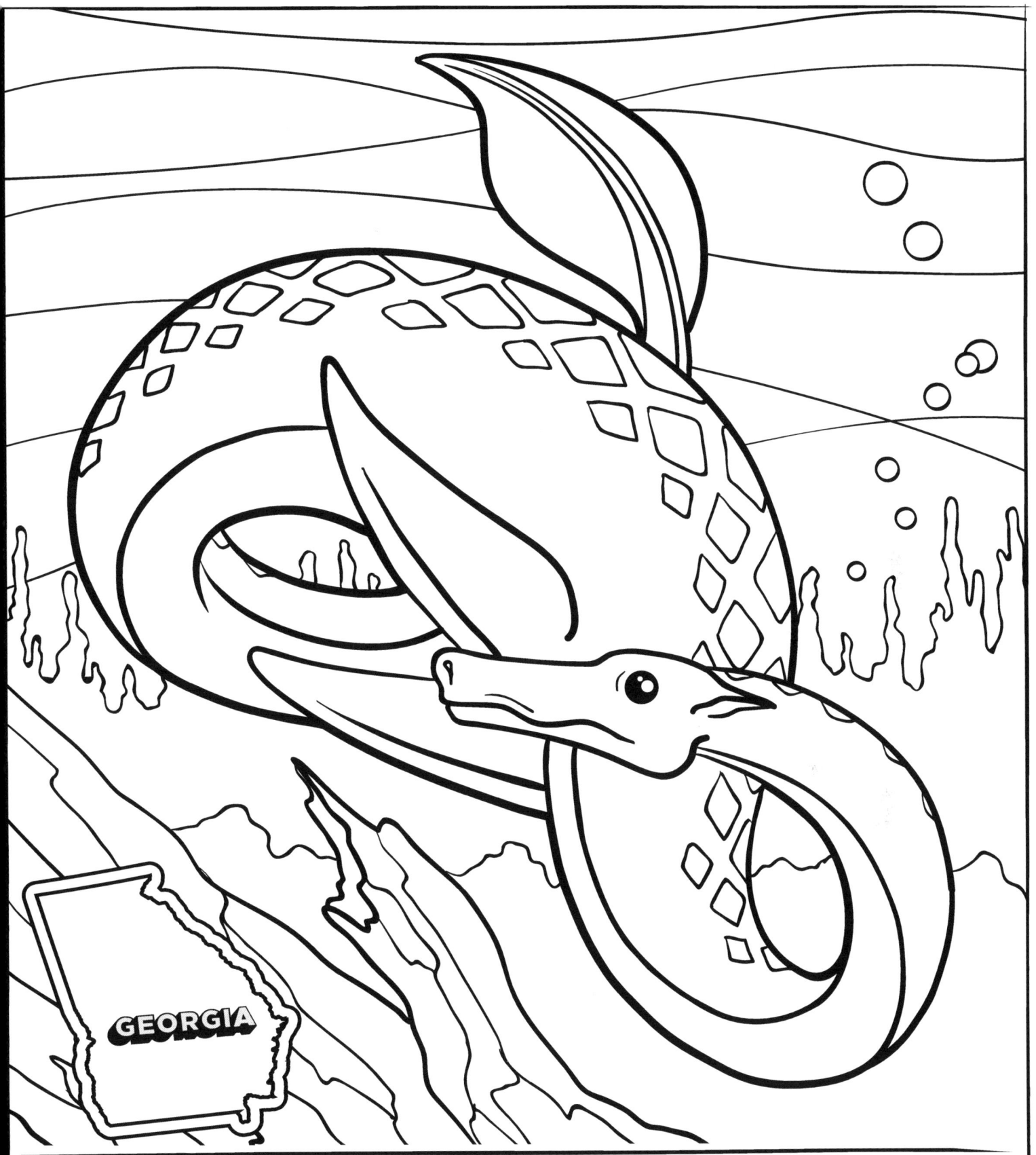

GEORGIA

Altamaha-ha Georgia 1830-Present

Stories about "Altie" have been around since before European explorers arrived. In 1830, Captain Delano of the schooner "Eagle" reported an animal 70-feet long and as big around as a large oak barrel, with an alligator-shaped head rising eight feet out of the water. Altie is said to have a dark smooth hide, tire-tread ridges on its back and a broad snout. The creature is said to travel fast enough to cause a "speedboat wake." Altie is one of the most sighted monsters in North America today.

Pterosaur **Hawaii** 1970-Present

If there is anywhere in the world you might find flying dinosaurs, Hawaii's climate would be it. With a 30-foot wingspan and brown, featherless, lizard-like skin, the Ptersaur has a horn on the back of its head and four wing fingers. There are continual sightings of large and small pterosaurs. One woman claims to regularly see smaller ones with long sharp beaks and a 3-4 foot wingspan that are more bat-like than bird-like. The Ptersaur's long tail is easily distinguished from its back legs because of the "diamond" on its tip.

Monsters & Cryptids in the United States of America © 2017 **VIGpublishing**

Sharlie AKA Slimey Slim Idaho 1920-Present

Thirty feet long with a dinosaur-type head and pronounced jaws, Slimy Slim has humps like a camel and a shell-like skin. In 1944 *Time* magazine ran an article saying that over 30 people, "including republicans and teatotalers," had spotted a creature with a scaly cylindrical body and a stumpy cow-like head. The monster became so popular in the area, that in 1954, the local newspaper held a contest to name the beast. "Sharlie" won and the sightings continued. The most recent one was reported in 2002.

ILLINOIS

The Enfield Horror Illinois 1973

At 9:30 p.m. on April 30th, 1973, Henry McDaniel heard scratching at his front door. Glancing through the window, he saw a 4 1/2-foot tall greyish creature with red/pink eyes as big as flashlights staring at him. It had a short body and 3 legs with two small, clawed arms coming from its breast area. Henry shot at it. It hissed like a wildcat and bounded away — 50-feet in 3 hops. When the police arrived they found doglike tracks in the yard that represented a 3-legged animal with one track slightly smaller.

Monsters & Cryptids in the United States of America © 2017 VIGpublishing

Beast of Busco Indiana 1898-1949

Oscar Fulk claimed to see an enormous snapping turtle in his lake in 1898. On March 2, 1949, it was spotted again and desribed as being the size of a car's roof and weighing 500 pounds. Its neck was as wide as a stovepipe and its head was the same size as a child's. A week later newspapers across the nation were running stories about sightings of the beast, and by March 14th, 3000 monster hunters had arrived. The town of Churubusco still holds its "Turtle Days" festival in June to celebrate this monster!

IOWA

Van Meter Visitor Iowa 1903

Described as a tall dark humanoid with bat wings, a beak and a horn on its head that emitted a blinding light, this creature haunted the downtown rooftops of local businesses and was seen by dozens of people. Over the course of a week, the town grew more and more fearful, and several people shot at the creature to no avail. Eventually men with rifles followed the creature to an abandoned mine where it called to a fellow creature in the depths. The monsters retreated into the mine under the hail of gunfire and never returned.

Monsters & Cryptids in the United States of America © 2017 VIGpublishing

KANSAS

Blue Albino Woman Kansas 1963-Present

Reportedly from Topeka, this albino woman had white hair and skin pale enough to appear blue-ish. A group of men accused her of being a witch and were said to have buried her alive, but hundreds of locals have seen her as recently as 2013. She's even been seen clawing herself from the earth in the Rochester Cemetary on several occasions. Described as a frail lady with a horrible blue-ish complexion and red eyes, some also say her teeth are pointed and that she will devour victims like a zombie... perhaps she is one.

Demon Leaper Kentucky 1880-Present

For over a century, generations of people in Old Louisville have seen, and shot at, what has been described as an agile winged monkey. Some say he's wearing a shiny suit, others say his skin shines. A bat-like creature, the Demon Leaper has leathery skin, wings and claws. It hops along the rooftops of downtown and is most often seen among the gargoyles and spires of the gothic Walnut Street Baptist Church. Some claim it is actually a gargoyle that has come to life.

The Grunch   Louisiana 1800-1900s

The Grunch are a stunted albino race that barely appear human. They are very small and can be mistaken for large hairless raccoons. They have red eyes, are clever and have a taste for blood. Named for Grunch Road, where a settlement of banished humans once lived, the Grunch use trained goats to lure people into the woods. It was said that if you see a loose goat on the side of the road, drive faster; the Grunch are hunting. Sightings have tapered off as their land has been developed in recent years and Grunch Road no longer exists.

Bigfoot Maine 1800-Present

Everyone knows Bigfoot. He's been glimpsed in most states, but Maine sightings have been documented since the 1800s. From a trapper who was beaten to death against a tree to sisters who lost their fishing haul to a couple of "hair-covered giants," the sightings of Bigfoot have persisted in Maine for decades. He's been described as "an immense African monkey," "a giant chimpanzee," and "a big hairy man." The reports keep coming, and we keep listening. There have even been reports in the last year.

Chessie **Maryland** 1977-Present

For decades people have been seeing a long, dark, snake-like creature in Chesapeake Bay. It seems to be anywhere from 25-40 feet long with a head the size of a football and a resemblance to a horse. Some sightings attribute flippers to the creature, but most witnesses claim that it undulates like a snake or eel through the water. In 1980 a photograph was taken of a creature that turned out to be a mantee. It was returned to the warmer waters of Florida, but it has returned several times. Maybe it wants to see Chessie too!

Dover Demon **Massachusetts** 1977-Present

First seen crawling on a wall by three teens in a car, the Dover Demon has an enormous "figure eight" or "hourglass shaped" head on a 4-foot tall, stick-like body. Possessing long limbs and large prehensile hands and feet that curl around rocks as it walks, the creature can walk upright, but it often travels on all fours or switches back and forth between the two modes of locomotion. It has eyes that glow, sometimes orange, sometimes green, and has no mouth or nose.

Dogman Michigan 1887-Present

Two lumberjacks saw a creature which they described as over six feet tall with a man's body and a dog's head. Sightings of the Dogman continued for decades in the Upper Peninsula. An incident in 1938 claimed that Robert Fortney was charged by a pack of five wild dogs and when he shot over their heads to scare them away, one stood its ground. Fortney shot again, and the lead dog, huge and black, stood up on its hind legs, stared him down with hateful blue eyes and walked away from him into the woods upright!

Wendigo **Minnesota** 1800-Present

Strongly associated with the winter, the north and extreme cold, the Wendigo is always hungry for human flesh. It is described as human shaped but gaunt to the point of skeletal, with grey skin. Its yellow eyes are deeply sunk in its head, and it has a long tongue in a mouth that is ragged and torn from constant eating. Some say it has antlers, others say it is a giant. Native Americans actively hunted the Wendigo well into the 20th century. Sightings continue to come in even today in Minnesota and parts of Canada.

Black-eyed Kids **Mississippi** 1996-Present

Since the mid-90s, reports have come in about children who knock on doors and windows begging to be let in late at night. With eyes downcast, the children (some appearing as young as five) ask for food or to use the phone or bathroom and get increasingly aggressive the longer they have to wait. Eventually the children look up to reveal that they have no whites to their eyes. Most people report an overpowering sense of fear which keeps them from opening the door. The "children" are reported to travel in small groups.

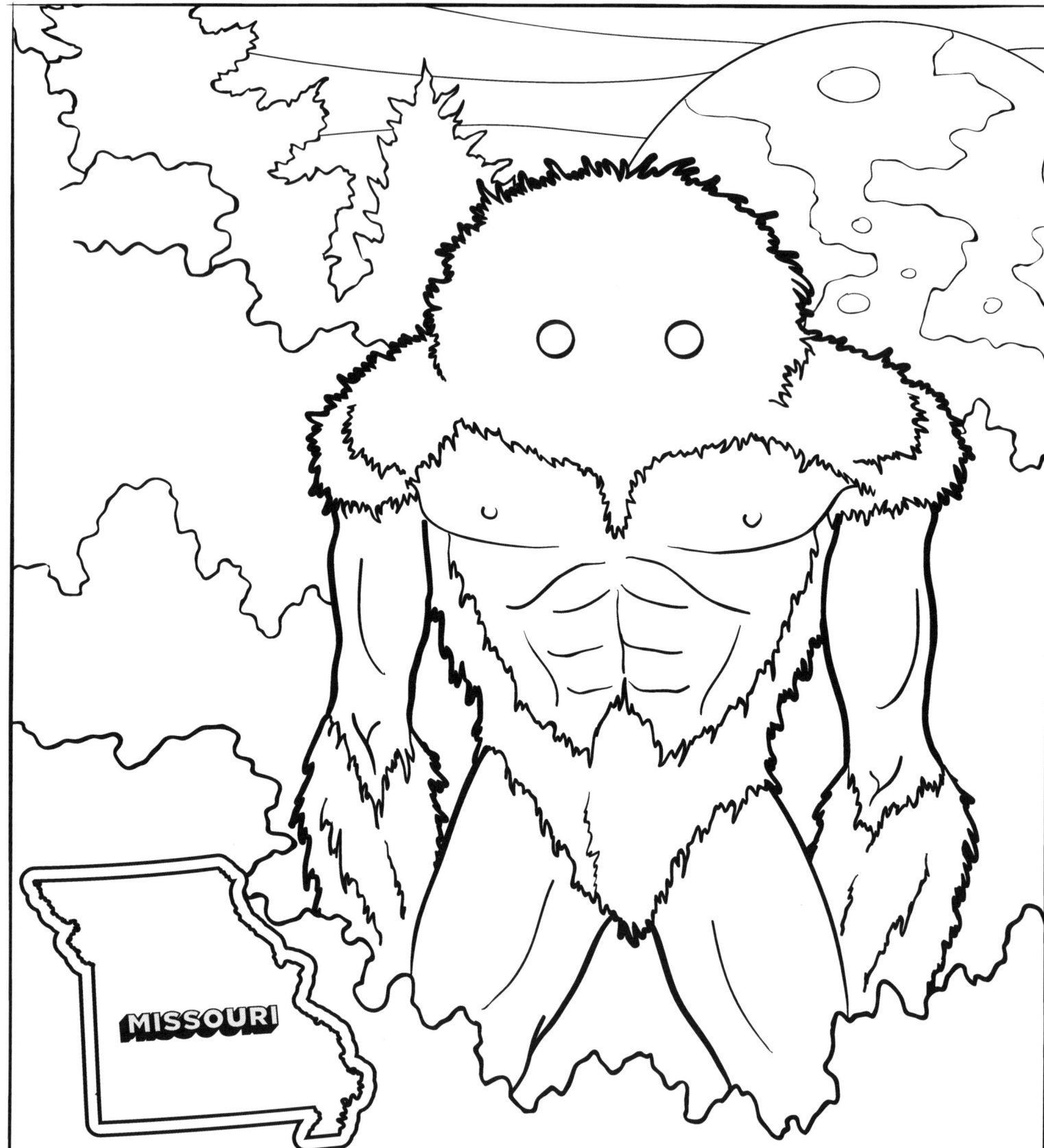

Momo Missouri 1950-Present

The name Momo is short for 'Missouri Monster,' and it is reported to have a large, pumpkin-shaped head with no neck, and red eyes. It is completely covered in black hair, 7 feet tall and emits a terrible odor. The creature is aggressive and chased 2 women into a car in 1971. It tried to get in until the horn scared it off. In 1972 some children witnessed it carrying a dead dog. Three days later during a prayer group at the same house, howls and growls in the yard caused the church members to flee in terror.

Shunka Warakin   Montana 1880-Present

A primitive wolf that has high shoulders sloping down like a hyena. It is believed that Ross Hall may have shot one that a local taxidermist stuffed in the 1880s. (Search 'Ringdocus' on the internet.) In 2006 an animal dubbed "The Creature of McCone County" killed over 120 livestock before being taken down by Montana Wildlife Services. It had orange, red and yellow fur as well as characteristics that were not common with any wolf species known. DNA analysis is still pending, but many think it is a Shunka Warakin.

NEBRASKA

Alkali Lake Monster **Nebraska** 1921-Present

Alkali Lake is now known as Walgren Lake. In most documented sightings, the creature thrashes its tail and roars to scare away intruders. It is over 40 feet long with greyish-brown rough skin. It looks longer and heavier than an aligator and has a rhinocerous horn growing between its eyes. It is rumored to smell awful. Some depictions have it with four legs, some with two legs and a flipper tail. There have been many sightings reported in the papers over the years, and the legend lives on.

Tahoe Tessie **Nevada** 1950-Present

With almost 200 square miles, Lake Tahoe stretches into California and is the 10th deepest lake in the world. Reports of sea serpents living within its depths go back centuries. From wake sightings where there are no boats, to surfacing humps or fin prints in the mud, witnesses differ substantially in what they claim to have seen. Some say Tessie looks a lot like the Loch Ness monster and others say she is a giant snake. Still others claim to have a seen a massive fish. Maybe there's more than one monster in the Nevada depths.

Wood Devils New Hampshire

Settlers in New Hampshire describe being surprised by these elusive creatures. They are said to have a slinky serpentine way about them. They avoid people and are exceptionally tall, thin, grey and hairy. Called wood devils, they are humanoid in shape. If they have been observed, they will hide behind a tree and move so that the tree is always between them and the viewer. Some will hold their ground until sure that they have been spotted and emit a piercing scream before running away at amazing speeds.

Jersey Devil New Jersey 1735-Present

The Pine Barrens is a place trackers get lost, and home to the famous Jersey Devil. A bipedal, winged creature with the head of a goat or horse, kangaroo haunches, a forked tail, clawed hands and cloven hooves, its first publicly recorded attack was on a trolley car in Haddon Heights in 1909. The Devil then flew across the Delaware river and was fired upon by the police. Statewide panic set in as schools and businesses were closed. Reports of home invasions, hoofprints on roofs, blood curdling cries and more continue to this day.

NEW MEXICO

Skinwalkers New Mexico

Generally believed to be a Native American medicine man, Skinwalkers have black hair, eyes that glow like an animal's and a nearly featureless face while transformed. They have long arms and go on all fours wearing the skin of the animal they wish to channel. When in animal form, they move stiffly and more unnaturally than the animal they are copying. Unlike a werewolf, Skinwalkers can change whenever they choose. Hairy biped sightings in the region are attributed to skinwalkers.

Alligators in the Sewers New York 1935-?

In 1935, the *New York Times* ran an article about several teens shoveling snow into a manhole. One noticed movement below and soon all were staring into the eyes of an alligator. They lassoed it with a clothesline and pulled it out. It snapped at the boys who then killed it with their shovels. The boys dragged it to a shop and found it weighed 125 lbs and was almost 8-feet long. Luckily the cold had made it sluggish. Then in 1937 Teddy May (the city's sewer superintendent) found and exterminated a colony of alligators with guns and poison.

Bladdenboro Beast North Carolina 1954-Present

Black and sleek, this vampire beast was seen by dozens of people in December 1954. It drained the blood from everything it came in contact with, especially dogs. It is said to have a cry like a baby screaming, weigh about 150 pounds and be 3-4 feet in length with a catlike face and and a bushy tail. By January 7th of '55, over 1000 people had come to hunt the beast but to no avail. In 2007, 60 goats were found with the blood drained from their bodies. Another man lost 10 dogs in two weeks. Large cat tracks were found at the scene.

Thunderbirds North Dakota

A Thunderbird is a creature from Native American mythology. In recent years, it has become the term used to describe any extremely large bird. Fossil records show that some teratorns had wingspans 18 foot wide and could be up to 8 feet tall! They were around before the dawn of man, but are they still here? Many people say yes. In 1977 a boy was picked up and carried 40 feet horizontally until the bird dropped him. More recently, a miltary police officer saw something as large as a hang glider flapping in the air near a base.

Loveland Frogs Ohio 1955-1972

In Loveland, Ohio, a witness saw three 4-foot tall bipeds. They were scaley and had frog-like heads with wrinkles where their hair should be. In 1972, an officer slammed on the brakes when he saw a crouched frog-like creature who then stood on two legs and bounded back to the river. Two weeks later another officer saw a similar creature and took a shot at it. Later that year a farmer saw the frogmen escape to the river and said they had large circular eyes, pale greenish-grey skin and mouths filled with sharp teeth.

Oklahoma Octopus Oklahoma

Although no freshwater octopi exist, sightings in Oklahoma trace back to the Native Americans, specifically in the Illinois and Vertigris rivers. More recently though, three lakes in Oklahoma have been home to the sightings. Witnesses report significantly sized tentacles breaking the water. Described as leathery reddish brown and the size of a horse, this creature has been blamed for the unusually high mortality rate and unexplained drownings in Oklahoma lakes. Keep in mind, an octopus can even walk on land for short periods...

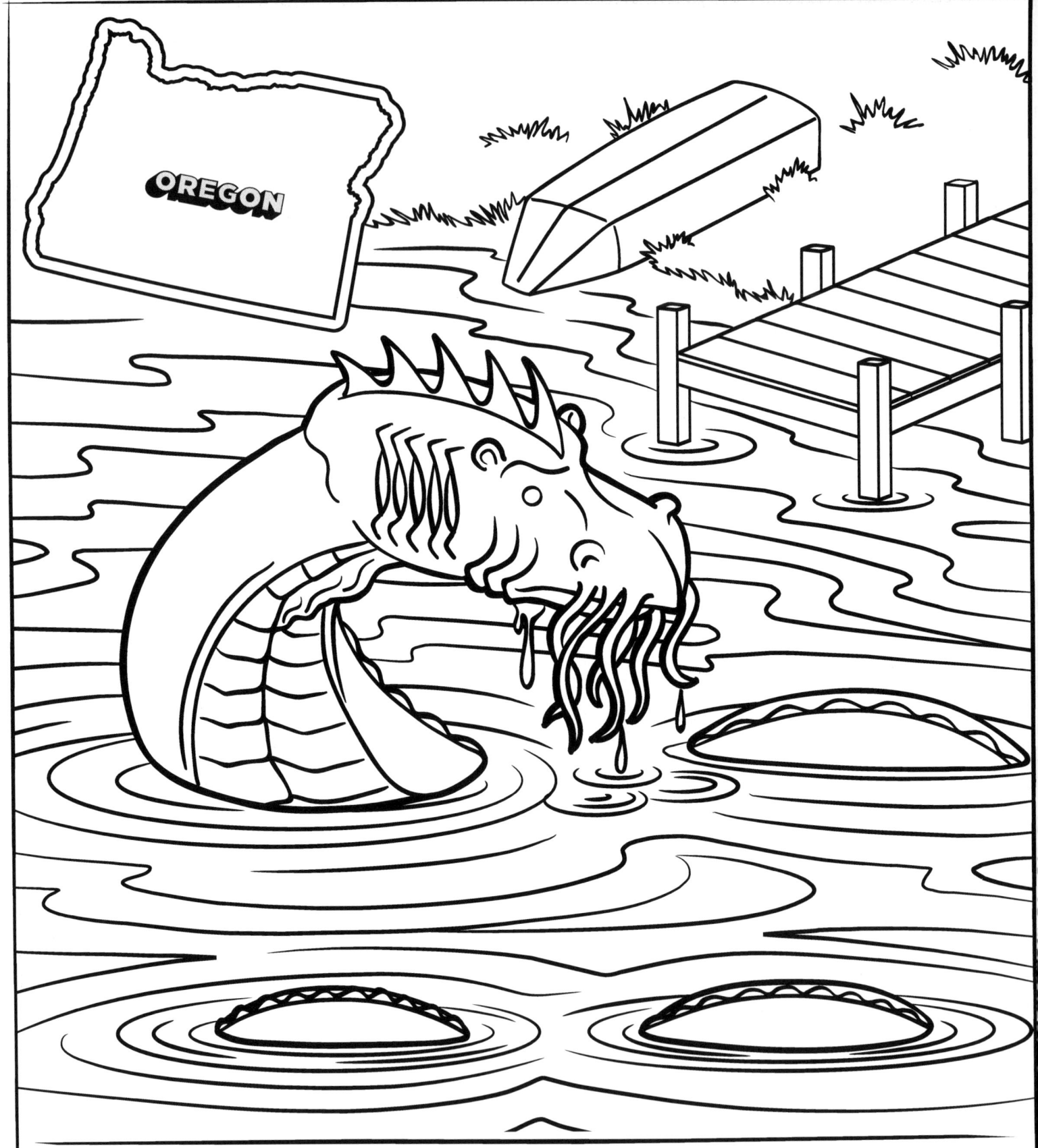

Wallowa Lake Monster Oregon 1885-Present

In Wallowa Lake, there have been sightings of a monster resembling a chinese dragon with the bellow of a cow. It is described as a long serpent with multiple humps, and horns on its head. Reports go as far back as the accounts of the Nez Perce Indians who refused to go near the water. The monster seems to have a 3-foot long head resembling a hippo or hog and a neck as big around as a man's waist. Reports have been coming in for centuries, and while "Wally" isn't seen as often as other cryptids, he's still there.

The Monster of Seltzer's Hole Pennsylvania 1893

Hundreds of dead livestock were found over the summer of 1893. Numerous witnesses saw something the size of a cow, but with shorter legs and a longer body. Its back was humped and ridged. It had a wing/fin/claw protruding from each of its shoulder blades and a long thick forked tail. Its tracks showed feet like a bear, but webbed. Its head was as large as a horse and covered with warts. It had a horn below the eyes and one on each side below the ears. Its eyes were as large as teacups, and its mouth large enough to hold a calf.

Puckwudgie Rhode Island

The Wampanoag Indians described 3-foot tall beings that are humanoid in appearance yet have enlarged fingers, ears and noses. They are grey skinned and seem to glow. Many people claim that their mischievous nature is responsible for the frequent deaths at the Fall-River-Freetown State Forest. They are reported to have quills on their back that they can smooth down or fluff up to resemble a porcupine. They dress in moss and other items from nature and use tools and weapons like bows or spears.

Lizardman **South Carolina** 1988-Present

Chris Davis was changing a tire near the swamps of Bishopville when he heard a noise. He barely got into his car when he was attacked by a creature 7-feet tall, covered in dark hair and greenish lizard skin. It had red eyes and black nails, and it aggressively tried to get in the car. He sped off with it on the roof and managed to shake it loose. Law enforcement found 14" long, 3-toed tracks at the site of the attack. Sighting reports have come in as recently as 2011.

SOUTH DAKOTA

Walking Sam/Big Man South Dakota 1980

For decades, people have seen a giant in a stovepipe hat and long coat peering through second story windows. Some reports say he has no face or mouth, yet police have taped his screams and have picked him up on thermal scanners. He is described as being between 9 and 15 feet tall, lanky and dressed in black. Police responded to the call of one family of witnesses, only to find them armed with knives and barricaded in their house with their cowering dogs under a fort made of furniture. Was this the origin of Slenderman?

Wampus Cat **Tennessee**

Scaring people in Northeast Tennessee for hundreds of years, the Wampus Beast is largely seen as an enormous panther or mountain lion with glowing yellow eyes. Stories abound concerning the origin of the beast, but one thing is constant. It has the mind of a human and the bloodlust of a beast. Some say it has human facial characteristics. Others say it is a Cherokee Skinwalker. Still others say it has six legs! Reports say it smells like a cross between a skunk and a wet dog, and it is rumored to have kidnapped children.

Lake Worth Goat-man Texas 1969-Present

The first report was by a couple who saw a half-man, half-goat fishy creature with fur and scales. Described as a bipedal humanoid with a long neck, it has the head of a goat or dog with a horn in the center. It has white hair and fish scales over its 7-foot tall body. The goat-fish-man has a pungent odor and has been known to be aggressive. On one occasion it hurled tires from a bluff at about a dozen people while howling and grunting. It has attacked cars and mangled sheep. Sightings continue to this day.

Bear Lake Monster Utah 1868-Present

Depending on who you ask, the description goes from a 30-50-foot undulating snake-like creature, to a monster with the face of a walrus without the tusks. One account was that it was all head, with two staring eyes as large as a wagon wheel and a mouth and nose like a great fish. Its arms seemed to come from where its ears would be and ended in great paws that left tracks 3-feet long and 2-feet wide. The back legs were bent like a kangaroo, and the hind end was like the tip of a fish. Could there be more than one beast?

VERMONT

Champ Vermont 1609-Present

Samuel De Champlain is said to have seen a creature with a head resembling a horse on a twenty foot neck. Over 300 reported sightings of the creature go back centuries to the Abenaki Indians who called the creature "Tatoskok." An 1819 newspaper article reports that Captain Crum sighted a serpentine monster with three teeth and eyes the color of peeled onions. It had a stripe of red around its neck and a white blaze on its forehead. To this day people claim to have seen something like a plesiosaur in the lake.

 Monsters & Cryptids in the United States of America © 2017 VIGpublishing

VIRGINIA

White Thang Virginia 1940-Present

Decades of reports and sightings in Boone County describe a quadruped as large as a bear, but with yellowish-white hair. It has a bear's skull with round, dark eyes set much lower on the head. It has two large, straight goat horns and a muzzle filled with huge sharp teeth. It also has raccoon hands, as opposed to a bear's flat paws, and some say, an opossum tail. But all reports agree it has an overwhelming stench of sulfur. Recent decades have dubbed the creature Sheepsquatch due to its matted white hair and horns.

WASHINGTON

Batsquatch *Washington* 1980-Present

After the eruption of Mt. St. Helen, people started seeing something they referred to as Batsquatch. The creature was 9-feet tall, with leathery bat-like wings that span 50-feet. Witnesses say it has a face like a wolf or a fox, yellow/red eyes and blue fur. Some reports have said it has purple skin, and many have stated that they have seen it fly from crevices in the mountain. In 2014 a teacher and her class saw something huge and dark zoom past their classroom window.

Mothman **West Virginia** 1965-Present

A man and his daughter skidded to a halt almost hitting a 7-foot tall, dull pewter grey creature in the middle of the road. They were stunned to see that it had no head, but rather two red glowing eyes set in its chest. It snapped open a pair of wings that spanned the width of the road and shot straight up into the night sky. After that, Mothman chasing cars was a regular report to local police. For two years the small town was plagued by sightings, hunters, and the media. Even the "Men in Black" questioned some witnesses.

Beast of Bray Road Wisconsin 1936-Present

The bear-sized beast is said to be over 3-feet tall on all fours and up to 7-feet tall when standing upright. One witness said it was the closest thing she ever saw to a werewolf. It has been seen eating roadkill and digging in Indian burial grounds with its sharp claws. There is a strong smell of decaying meat about it. With an athletic build and shaggy hair, it has a wolf-like face with bright yellow eyes and pointed ears. One person said it growled "Gadara", which many believe refers to Jesus healing the possessed man in Gadara.

Cannibal Pygmies Wyoming

The Shoshone Indians of Wyoming spoke of "tiny people eaters" before settlers came to their land. Supposedly only 2-3-feet tall, these aggressive Nimerigar warriors were feared for their tiny bows and poisoned arrows. In 1932 a San Pedro Mountain miner found a small mummy in a rock face that he'd blasted. The American Museum of Natural History tested it extensively and reported it to be a perfectly formed 65-year old man with a full set of canine teeth. Since then, the remains have been "reclassified" as an infant and "lost."

A sample coloring page of Pickman's Model from *Cthulhu's Coloring Book & Necronomicon of Sunny Day Doings*. Now with backgrounds and more pages to color! New version available on Amazon.com 9/1/2017.

Here's a sample coloring page from the *Mr. Cthulhu Presents: Space Aliens & Flying Objects in the United States of America*, Coloring Book. Coming to Amazon.com in 2018.

Available NOW from VIGpublishing.com

Mr. Cthulhu Presents:

CTHULHU'S COLORING BOOK & NECRONOMICON
OF SUNNY DAY DOINGS

Coloring book #1

SECOND EDITION! New cover, and more pages of fun! The stars are aligned and this tome of activities has arisen. Word games, mazes, puzzles and dot-to-dots punctuate plenty of coloring pages featuring horrors out of time that await your crayons! New version available 9/1/17.

Pages of creatures from the depths of R'lyeh wait for you to open the portal to *Cthulhu's Coloring Book & Necronomicon of Sunny Day Doings...* if you dare.

CREEPY, but Kid Friendly FUN

Coming SOON from VIGpublishing.com

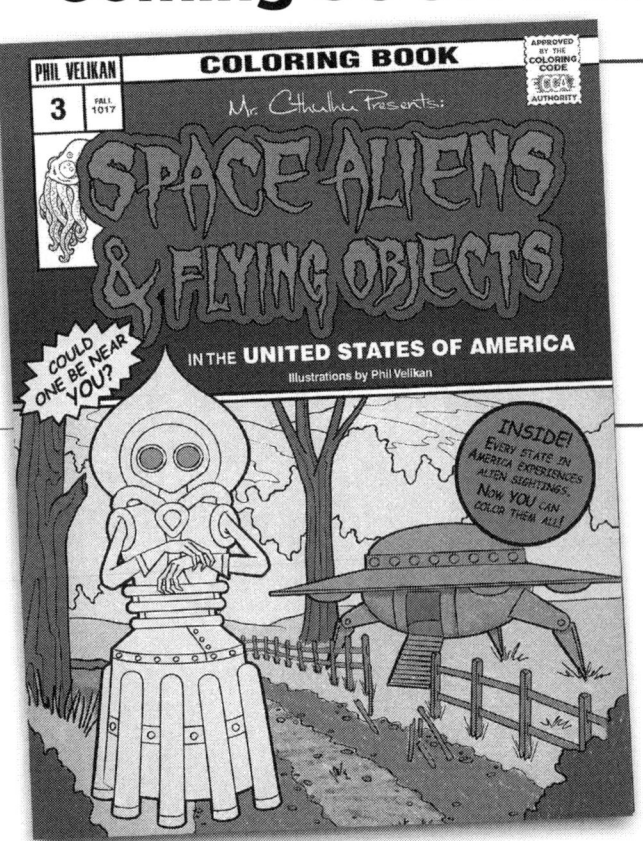

Mr. Cthulhu Presents:

SPACE ALIENS & FLYING OBJECTS
IN THE UNITED STATES OF AMERICA

Coloring book #3

In our United States, there have been reports of aliens and UFOs everywhere! From sightings to close encounters, you'll find the *Space Aliens & Flying Objects in the United States of America* coloring book fascinating.

Every one of the 50 states included has its own page with the state, encounter, dates, and a large illustration based on eyewitness accounts for you to color! Available 2018

Printed in Great Britain
by Amazon

58481617R00034